For Jasper, who is a force of nature
—L.S.

For Cosmo and Misha
—J.I.

Published in the United States by Random House Children's Books, a division of Random House, Inc., New York.

Random House and the colophon are registered trademarks of Random House, Inc.

Visit us on the Web! www.randomhouse.com/kids

Educators and librarians, for a variety of teaching tools, visit us at www.randomhouse.com/teachers

Library of Congress Cataloging-in-Publication Data
Snyder, Laurel.
Good night, laila tov / by Laurel Snyder ; illustrated by Jui Ishida. — 1st ed.
p. cm.
Summary: During a family camping trip a brother and sister enjoy exploring nature, and each night they hear the English and
Hebrew phrases for good night from the waves, wind, or grass.
ISBN 978-0-375-86868-9 (trade) — ISBN 978-0-375-96868-6 (lib. bdg.) — ISBN 978-0-375-89939-3 (ebook)
[1. Stories in rhyme. 2. Camping—Fiction. 3. Family life—Fiction. 4. Nature—Fiction. 5. Bedtime—Fiction. 6. Jews—
United States—Fiction. 7. Humorous stories.] I. Ishida, Jui, ill. II. Title. III. Title: Laila tov.
PZ7.S6851764Goo 2012 [E]—dc22 2010037761

MANUFACTURED IN CHINA
10 9 8 7 6 5 4 3 2 1
First Edition

Good night, laila tov

By Laurel Snyder

Illustrated by Jui Ishida

RANDOM HOUSE 🏠 NEW YORK

The sun was up. The day was bright!
It filled our room with yellow light.

It woke us both, so right away . . .

We grabbed our things, were on our way.

We drove out to the oceanside.
The sand was hot. The waves were wide.

Tall grasses swayed. The salty air
Was soft and still and everywhere.

And the waves whispered . . .

Good night, laila tov. . . .

We found a place so great and green,
The deepest field we'd ever seen.

We gathered berries, sweet and red,
As shadows circled overhead.

And the sky sang . . .

Good night, laila tov. . . .

We helped our parents plant some trees.

We found some mice.

We found some bees!

Then suddenly,
The rain came down.
In plips and plops
It hit the ground.

And the storm shushed . . .

Good night, laila tov . . .

We climbed into the sandy car
With all our treasures in a jar.

We stopped for dinner, stopped to see . . .

Stopped again so I could pee.

And the road rumbled . . .

Good night, laila tov. . . .

When we got home, the sky was black.
The cat was happy we'd come back.

And though the day was done and gone,
Somehow the lights were all still on!

Good night, laila tov. . . .